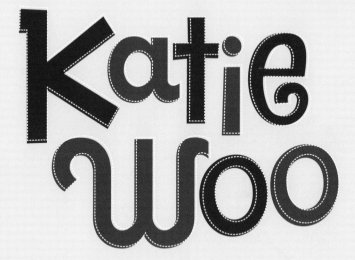

Katie Woo

and Her BIG Ideas

by Fran Manushkin

illustrated by Tammie Lyon

capstone

Katie Woo is published by Picture Window Books
A Capstone Imprint
1710 Roe Crest Drive
North Mankato, MN 56003
www.capstonepub.com

Library of Congress Cataloging-in-Publication Data
Manushkin, Fran.
  Katie Woo and her big ideas / by Fran Manushkin; illustrated by Tammie Lyon.
     p. cm. — (Katie Woo)
  Summary: Combines four previously published stories, including Katie in the kitchen, Katie saves the Earth, Katie's lucky birthday, and Katie's new shoes, in which Katie does her best to be considerate and helpful.
  ISBN 978-1-4795-2026-8 (pbk.)
  1. Woo, Katie (Fictitious character)—Juvenile fiction. 2. Helping behavior—Juvenile fiction. 3. Chinese Americans—Juvenile fiction. [1. Helpfulness—Fiction. 2. Conduct of life—Fiction. 3. Chinese Americans—Fiction.] I. Lyon, Tammie, ill. II. Title. III. Series: Manushkin, Fran. Katie Woo.
  PZ7.M3195Kbek 2013
  813.54—dc23   2012049913

Photo Credits
Greg Holch, pg. 96; Tammie Lyon, pg. 96

Designer: Kristi Carlson

Printed in the United States of America in North Mankato, Minnesota.
062013   007449R

Table of Contents

Katie Saves the Earth

"Earth Day is coming," said Miss Winkle. "How can we keep the Earth green?"

"We can paint it green," said Katie Woo. "But we will need lots of paint."

"That is not what I mean," said Miss Winkle. "I want to keep the Earth green by taking care of the plants and trees. They need clean air and water."

"I know what to do," said JoJo. "We can fix leaks in our sinks. Then we won't waste water."

"That's a great idea," said Miss Winkle.

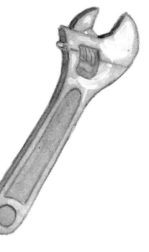

"We can reuse things," said
Pedro. "My little brother sleeps in
my old crib."

"I want to do something great for
Earth Day," said Katie.

"I'm sure you will," said Miss
Winkle.

"I know what to do!" said Katie.
"I'll have a yard sale. My friends can
bring things for people to reuse.
That will make the Earth happy."

On Earth Day, Katie put her old
toys on the lawn.

"Are you sure you don't want
them?" asked her mom.

"I'm sure!" said Katie.

JoJo brought a teapot without a top and a broken lamp.

"Who will want those?" wondered Katie.

Pedro brought torn jeans and
books.

"Nobody will want those either,"
worried Katie.

Soon the first shopper arrived. It was Miss Winkle!

She told Pedro, "I can turn your jeans into a tote bag for my books."

Pedro's little
brother Paco grabbed
Katie's old elephant.

"Hey!" yelled Katie.
"I put that outside by
mistake."

Katie ran inside and put the
elephant back on her bed.

Then Katie went back outside. "I hope more people come," she said.

But nobody did.

"What can we do?" Katie asked her friends.

Pedro's dad picked up JoJo's
lamp. "I can fix this and use it at
work," he said.

"Yay!" yelled JoJo.

"Pedro's books look great," said
JoJo. "I can take them home to
read."

"That's terrific!" yelled Pedro.
"All of my stuff is gone!"

"I can put my
paint brushes in
JoJo's teapot,"
said Katie.

"Yay!" cheered
JoJo. "Now all of
my stuff is gone, too."

"But none of mine is gone."
Katie sighed.

Just then, little Paco fell down.
He cried and cried. Katie patted
him, but he kept crying.

"Poor Paco," she said. "I have an
idea!"

Katie ran into her house. Then
she returned, holding something
behind her back.

"Surprise!" said Katie. "Here is
my elephant!"

Paco hugged it and smiled.

"When I was little," said Katie,
"it made me feel better, too."

"That is smart reusing," said
Katie's mom. "But are you sure it's
okay?"

"I'm sure!" Katie smiled. "Paco
and I are both happy."

The birds were singing, and the air smelled sweet.

"The Earth looks happy, too," said Katie.

And it did!

EARTH DAY ❁
YARD SALE -
TODAY!

Katie's Lucky Birthday

Katie's birthday was coming.

"I'm having a party at school!" she told her friends. "I can't wait."

"I know how you feel," said JoJo. "Birthdays are the best!"

"My mom measures me on my birthday," said JoJo. "It's fun to see how much I've grown."

Pedro said, "On my birthday, my dad makes me blueberry pancakes. My birthday is in August, so there are plenty of blueberries."

"There is no school in August,"
said Katie. "So you can't have a
party at school."

"Nope," said Pedro. "I never do."

The sun was shining on Katie's birthday. Her mom and dad gave her a bright red sweater.

"Red is my lucky color!" Katie said. "It means my birthday will be perfect."

"I made a special treat for your class party," said Katie's mom.

"What is it?" asked Katie.

"It's a surprise," said her mom. "You'll find out later."

When class began, Miss Winkle
announced, "Today is Katie's
birthday. She will be my POD."

"What's a POD?" asked Barry, the new boy.

"It means Person of the Day," said Pedro.

"Katie can start by leading the Pledge," said Miss Winkle. Katie led the Pledge in a nice, loud voice.

Katie was also the line leader at recess. "I wish it was my birthday every day," she said.

"Well," said Pedro, "you have 364 unbirthdays. Today is one of mine."

The twins, Ellie and Max, said,
"Our birthday is double the fun."

"Double the fun?" repeated Katie.
She looked at Pedro. "That gives me
an idea!"

During art, Katie asked the twins to help her paint a poster. "It's a secret," Katie told them.

"We're great at keeping secrets," said Ellie.

"Except from each other," added Max.

"What are you painting?" asked Pedro.

"Oh, nothing," said Katie.

Pedro laughed. "When you say nothing, it means you are up to something!"

Finally, it was time for Katie's party. Her mom came with the special treat. The plate was huge!

"My mother is up to something, too!" said Katie.

The class gasped when they saw
the treat. It was a giant rose made of
strawberries.

"It's red! My lucky color!" Katie
said.

"HAPPY BIRTHDAY KATIE" was spelled out in blueberries.

"Blueberries! My favorite!" shouted Pedro.

"Katie's mom searched until she found them," said JoJo.

"Now, it's time for another surprise,"
announced Katie.

The twins held up Katie's secret
poster. It said, "Happy Unbirthday,
Pedro and Everyone Else!"

Pedro couldn't stop smiling.

The class sang "Happy Birthday" to Katie. Then everyone ate the strawberries and blueberries.

On the way home, Katie told JoJo
and Pedro, "My birthday party was
totally perfect."

"For me too!" added Pedro. "I felt like a POD."

"That's because you are!" Katie said.

Then the three of them ran home. It was triple the fun!

Katie's New Shoes

"Something is wrong with my toes," said Katie Woo. "They hurt when I walk or run. They hurt when I wiggle them, too. I think I have the ouches!"

"Your toes are fine," said Katie's mom. "Your shoes are the problem. You are growing so fast, they don't fit you anymore."

"Uh-oh," Katie groaned. "I'd better slow down! If I keep growing fast, my feet will be as big as a horse's or an elephant's!"

"No way," said Katie's dad. "I promise you will always have human feet."

"Good!" said Katie. "I like being human."

Katie told Pedro and JoJo about
her big toes.

"My toes are so
big, they poked a
hole in my shoes,"
bragged Pedro.

"My shoes are
falling apart, too," said JoJo.

Katie, Pedro, and JoJo went to
Super Shoes with their moms. The
store was huge!

It had sneakers and boots and party shoes. It had shoes with sparkles and shoes with wheels.

It had boxes of shoes all the way to the ceiling!

"I want speedy shoes," said Pedro. "Shoes for running fast!"

"I want bouncy shoes," said JoJo. "Shoes for jumping high!"

Katie said, "I want shoes with pizzazz!"

"What's pizzazz?" asked JoJo.

"It means they look great!" said Katie.

"We want different things," said
JoJo. "I'm sure we won't like the same
shoes."

Katie tried on shoes with buckles
and bows and straps and zippers.
Soon the boxes were piled high.

"None of these has pizzazz," said
Katie, sighing.

"I wish I were a cat," said Katie. "Cats have their own furry shoes."

"But cats have to eat mice," said Katie's mom.

"Yuck!" Katie moaned. "Never mind!"

A little girl near Katie was crying.

"She doesn't like trying on shoes," said her mom.

"Shoes can be fun!" Katie told the little girl. But the girl kept crying.

"Look!" Katie said to the girl.

She put baby shoes on her hands and made them dance and talk like puppets.

The little girl giggled and let her
mom try on some shoes.

"Thank you!" said the mom as
Katie danced away.

"Will I ever find the perfect shoes?"
Katie sighed.

"Yes," said her mom. "Just like
Cinderella!"

Katie tried on her sixteenth pair of shoes. "Hey," she said, smiling. "These are IT!"

"Do they have pizzazz?" asked Katie's mom.

"Tons of it!" said Katie. "And my toes are happy!"

Katie danced over to JoJo, saying, "Look! I found the perfect shoes."

"Surprise!" JoJo said. "We picked the same ones."

"Wow!" Katie said. "We both have pizzazz."

"Sure," agreed Pedro. "But my shoes are the fastest."

"Race you home!" Katie said. And off they went!

They passed the little girl. She was showing off her new shoes.

"Shoes are fun!" she shouted.

Katie agreed. "When my toes are happy, I'm happy."

And she kept on running!

Katie in the Kitchen

One day, Katie's mom said, "I'm going next door. Mrs. West has the flu, so I'm going to bring her some soup."

"Can I come and help?" asked Katie.

"That's not a good idea," said her mom. "You might catch the flu too."

Katie's dad was in the garage fixing his car.

"Can I help you?" Katie asked. "I love fixing things."

"No," said her dad. "These tools are tricky. You might get hurt."

Katie went back inside, feeling sad.

"I want to help, but nobody will let me," she said to herself. "I know what to do! I'll make dinner. Mom and Dad will be so happy!"

"Mom loves spaghetti," said Katie. "And so do I."

Katie filled a pot with water, three boxes of spaghetti, four cans of tomato sauce, and a jar of olives.

"I think that's enough," Katie said.
"Turning on the stove is a no-no, so
Mom can cook this when she comes
back."

"Now I'll make cookies," decided Katie. "Dad loves cookies, and so do I."

Katie poured a bag of flour into a bowl, added two bags of chocolate chips, and stirred it as hard as she could.

Flour flew everywhere. "It's snowing!" Katie shouted.

She wrote her name in flour on the floor. Then she slipped, and — oops! She fell down.

"I hurt my knees." Katie sighed.
She put on a few Band-Aids.

"These new Band-Aids are fun,"
she said. So she put a few on her
nose too.

"Mom can bake the cookies when she comes home," Katie decided. "Maybe she can clean up the floor too."

Katie called Pedro and bragged, "Guess what? I'm making dinner tonight."

"Cool!" Pedro shouted. "I'm reading a great ghost story. I hope there aren't any ghosts in your house."

"No way!" Katie said. "Goodbye!"

"I'm not scared of ghosts," Katie told herself.

Just then she heard a weird sound.

"That's not a ghost!" she decided.

But just in case, she turned on all the lights. She also put on her mom's robe to make herself feel bigger.

Suddenly, a storm
began! Lightning flashed!
Thunder boomed!

"Storms don't scare
me!" Katie said.

She put on her dad's hat to make herself feel braver. The thunder grew louder — and closer.

"Yow!" Katie yelled, and she hid in the closet.

Soon she heard a loud noise.

THUMP! THUMP! THUMP!

"It's the ghost!" Katie moaned.

Slowly the closet door began opening.

"EEEE!" screamed Katie.

"EEEE!" yelled the ghost.

"Mom!" yelled Katie.

"Katie!" shouted her mom. "You scared me to death!"

"And this house," said Katie's mom. "It looks like an earthquake hit it."

"It was a ghost!" said Katie quickly.

"Really?" said Katie's mother. "Are you sure it wasn't Hurricane Katie?"

"Maybe," Katie confessed.

"But supper is almost ready," Katie bragged. "I've done most of the work."

"Someone's making cookies!" said Katie's dad. "My favorite."

"I'm so glad I could help!" said Katie. "Just ask me — anytime!"